## About the Author

Claire started writing as a child to put some magic in their world; it felt like living a thousand different lives all at once. Later, they realised it was a way to cope with ADHD and the intense emotional bursts. What couldn't be said was inked on paper until this book was born.

# Faded Words of Lifelong Stories

Claire Zucchetta

Faded Words of Lifelong Stories

Olympia Publishers
*London*

www.olympiapublishers.com
OLYMPIA PAPERBACK EDITION

Copyright © Claire Zucchetta 2024

The right of Claire Zucchetta to be identified as author of this work has been asserted in accordance with sections 77 and 78 of the Copyright, Designs and Patents Act 1988.

**All Rights Reserved**

No reproduction, copy or transmission of this publication may be made without written permission.
No paragraph of this publication may be reproduced, copied or transmitted save with the written permission of the publisher, or in accordance with the provisions of the Copyright Act 1956 (as amended).

Any person who commits any unauthorised act in relation to this publication may be liable to criminal prosecution and civil claims for damage.

A CIP catalogue record for this title is available from the British Library.

ISBN: 978-1-80439-903-3

This is a work of fiction.
Names, characters, places and incidents originate from the writer's imagination. Any resemblance to actual persons, living or dead, is purely coincidental.

First Published in 2024

Olympia Publishers
Tallis House
2 Tallis Street
London
EC4Y 0AB

Printed in Great Britain

# Dedication

I dedicate this book to my insecure inner child.

# Acknowledgements

I would like to thank the many people who contributed to this collection with their mentorship, emotional support or simply by being around as a source of inspiration:

– Palmerston North City Library for the opportunity to contribute to *Versions* and *Versions Tuatoru*, two collections of stories from local artists, in which *Kim and Lee* and *Time is Passing* were first published.

– Zak and Cameron for revivifying my author's dying flame by introducing me to their own work as writers.

– Warren for his amazing journey: writing poems throughout his life and starting his novels at eighty years old.

– My D&D and Ten Candles crew for being awesome individuals that give life to my stories and inspire others.

– Nim and Tiliana for being my first reviewers and accepting to read the drafts of my poems or stories.

– Caio for his love, support and amazing brain, who had the wonderful idea to gift me Neil Gaiman's *Trigger Warning* and *Fragile Things*.

– Lucas for the enriching conversations about world building and character creation.

– Micaiah, beautiful human, love of my life, husband and friend, for being the wind beneath my wings, pushing me to write and embrace my creative side. I love you forever and always.

# PREFACE

I started working on *Faded Words of Lifelong Stories* after regrouping all my French-written short stories in a collection, *Descente en Enfer (Descent to Hell)*. I thought, *Why not do the same with what I wrote in English?* My native language being French, I always feared people would mock me for my grammar or spelling mistakes. I remember submitting a story to my English teacher with fear freezing my veins, only to be congratulated for my creativity and my use of the language. I did not have other opportunities to write stories in English until I arrived here in Aotearoa in 2018. After only two weeks in the land of the long white cloud, I met my now-husband, Micaiah, to whom I started writing poems. What a difficult exercise it is, versing in another language! First, because my accent doesn't allow me to properly assess when words rhyme or not; second, because my imagery and idioms are inherently linked to my French roots; and finally, because I had to use a dictionary! When I started dating Micaiah, I was working on short novels—mediocre ones. We instantly dived into discussions in which I would describe plots, worlds and characters. I fell in love with his passion and his interest in my art. Later, we participated in a writing workshop at the City Library in Palmerston North. For the first time, I let a stranger read my story and publish it in a collection. I felt so validated! It motivated me to improve my skills in English, and I did so during my first Dungeons and Dragons campaign, based on a high-fantasy novel that I never got the strength to finish, *Le Dernier Mage (The Last Mage)*. What an adventure! Then, another of my short stories, *Time is Passing,* got published by the City Library. It was at that time that I met Zak and Cameron. Reading their work made me realise that we all have our unique voice and distinctive ways of arranging words into stories. I resonated with Zak's slam poetry and voyaged into Cameron's plays and short stories with pure delight. I was finally ready to invest in my own writing. And as Neil Gaiman does in his short story collections, I would like to end this preface with anecdotes about each of the texts compiled here.

# 1
# KIM AND LEE

This story is the fruit of the very first writing workshop I attended, held by Sean Monaghan at the City Library. Here is what Sean wrote on the back cover of *Versions*, the collection of words written by local authors:

> *"Same starting point, different versions. What if a bunch of writers took the same opening premise and wrote something from that? Kim and Lee are trapped in Turakina and need to get back to Palmy. Kim has a guitar, and Lee has a book. Find out what happens next, according to eight writers."*

It was a wonderful adventure and incredibly enriching to see fellow writers talking about their inspirations, their struggles and their successes. For me, *Kim and Lee* was a journey in itself. It was easy to get the main idea, the vibe, but oh-so-hard to properly use English and give life to my characters. I repeatedly read the final draft, unsure if I would have the courage to submit it, so scared of my foreign voice. And it was published! Just like that! But then, I had the dreadful experience of the public launch, reading out loud what I had written. I got so scared that my palms were still sweating when I stuffed myself with the cheese and crackers offered at the end of the event. Nobody cared about my accent, the whole crowd was just as wholesome as Sean had been during the workshop. I came home sick because of my lactose intolerance, but motivated to embrace new paths in my writing journey!

# 2
# TIME IS PASSING

I have encountered the use of second-person point of view in a genius novel called *The Fifth Season* by N K Jemisin. Then, I realised that I was using it during our Dungeons and Dragons sessions, to describe to my players what they were seeing, experiencing or feeling in the game. In an Role Playing Game (RPG) context, it does make sense for a Dungeon Master (DM) to describe things from the second-person point of view, as you are the mind behind the story, but you have to immerse your players in the world you've built. From their perspective, the story would be told from the first-person point of view, and you could choose to use the third-person to describe what the character sees, experiences or feels. I thought it was always better to directly connect with the player, not just their in-game character. Anyhow, it became a habit to write stories that way, and when I started *Time is Passing*, I automatically used "you" to link my protagonist with the reader. As for the idea, it was guided by the *Versions Tuatoru*'s theme *Changing Seasons*. Once again, the City Library offered an opportunity to share a part of me with the world, and I was most grateful. I decided to write about the suffering of time flying by, youth disappearing in wrinkles but not from our hearts. I am sure that some will relate to the bullying and rejection, to the feeling of being queer in a world where you don't fit; and to them, I will say that you are loved and valid. I acknowledge your existence, as I have mine, after years of self-inflicted pain trying to fit in a mould. Now I can say what I am with confidence: I will never dimmish myself for others' comfort, and I will empower those around me who seek a community of like-minded people. Labels matter as they foster a sense of belonging that we all crave for. Be kind to others. Be kinder to yourself.

# 3
# MICAIAH

First poem I wrote to my at-the-time Kiwi boyfriend. I remember exactly where and when: alone on my single bed in my Milverton Avenue flat, in the middle of the day during the Christmas break. I had arrived in Palmy only a couple of weeks prior and started my internship at Massey University, only to be told that everyone would leave for the holidays. On the opposite side of the world, loneliness hit me like a storm: I had no friends, no family and no one to spend Christmas or New Year's Eve with. I opened Tinder, and matched with a bunch of uninteresting dudes, until one profile attracted my eyes: a blurry picture of a "goofball" in a racoon onesie. *Goofball, what an interesting way to describe oneself in a dating app bio*, I thought. We matched and started seeing each other. This poem bloomed from our first *I Love You*, on the 6th of January 2019. I was terrified because, for the first time in my life, a man was committing himself to me, declaring his love and showing vulnerability. I was impressed too, of his courage, his confidence and the trust he had in the authenticity of his feelings for me. Like many of us, I had been hurt in the past; like many of us, I am the result of my past traumas. *Men are dangerous, men take what they want and leave.* The little voice of self-preservation was loud and vicious, but I shut it down. *Micaiah is kind, loving and imperfect; so are you. He will hurt you, and you will hurt him, such is the price of love, only worth paying if you both tend to each other's wounds through communication, affection, and care.* I followed this instinct. I chose him, and so began our journey. As I'm writing this, I look at my opal engagement ring and my wedding band: how grateful I am for those past five years and the many yet to come.

# 4
# I AM BROKEN

In July 2019, I was travelling with my dad and brother, away from Palmy. We were in Rotorua. The day before, I crossed a line: persuaded of being right, tired of seeing my partner suffering from a situation that I thought to be so easily solved, I made a phone call, bypassing him. I realised the mess I'd created and, for the first time, I feared our relationship would end. Seeking comfort and advice, I contacted his sister, explaining her the situation, what I had done and how I felt. Her words carved my flesh so deeply that it reopened wounds of past insecurities. *Selfish. Arrogant. Controlling.* Words that were once used to hurt me, long forgotten in time, surfaced like a Leviathan in the dark ocean of my soul. I cried myself to sleep that night. The next day, I called my friend Kevin and cried some more. Being so far away from Micaiah made it even worse, as I couldn't communicate properly, read his body language or simply hold him and apologise. Instead, I wrote this poem.

# 5
# MR LYCHEE

Going from an open relationship to polyamory was no easy journey. We had to completely unhinge the stones of our home and rearrange them as we saw fit, according to our fears, needs and boundaries. Was it for the emotional connection? The physical intimacy? It took us several months to find terms on which we could both thrive, and if new partners were to join, they would feel welcomed and valued as human beings with fears, needs and boundaries, as equals. Polyamory is a wonderful adventure that allowed me to meet diverse people and connect with them. It has taught me a lot about myself and reaffirmed my deep love for my husband. *Mr Lychee* is not a praise for our polyamory – as I believe everyone should choose the type of relationship that best suits them, but rather a reminder that we have all suffered and that human connection can bring us inner peace. Often, friends told me, that they can't create a deep connection with multiple people, that it is already so hard to let down your guard. To that, I answered that having only one deep connection – your partner – can lead to emotional co-dependency. You don't have to romantically or sexually be involved to connect with another person. Friends and family are a good example, asexual relationships another one. We have so much to learn from others and it makes me sad that some miss opportunities out of fear of being judged, mocked or rejected. Easy for me to say, I have ADHD, so my emotional boundaries are almost absent, and I show my vulnerability recklessly: people share with me their darkest secrets and insecurities, usually ending the conversation with "It felt so good! You are so easy to talk to!" The downside of that superpower is that I give my trust to people who don't take care of me, and I end up being hurt. However, I still hold my position: contact with others enriches us, showing our true self should be what we aim for, and our wounds are part of who we are, not something to be ashamed of.

# 6
# FLESH AND STONE

The longest short story I have written so far, inspired by a Ten Candles (TCs) session. For those who don't know what TCs is, it's a horror tabletop RPG in which nobody survives. The DM gives a prompt describing the situation and the threat that the players are facing: "*they*", an unknown and undefined malevolent menace that will be shaped by the creative minds of the players during the game. During the preparation phase, participants write down traits on multiple pieces of paper and exchange them to create their characters. One player must give one to the DM for them to flesh out the threat. I received the following: "I've seen *them* turn stone into flesh." I loved reacting to what my friends came up with, everything was improvised, quick-paced, pleasing for my ADHD brain. Game sessions are usually six-hours long and full of plot twists. *Flesh and stone* was the most serious game we had, even though it included a flamingo sex fantasy, evil healing booze and rivers of blood. Some of my players read the story and told me it felt like a parallel universe where their characters were dealing with the same situation but without the randomness of their chaotic minds, only pure horror and dread. It made me happy, that's what I was going for!

# 7
# THE SCARABS OF TIME

After Caio, my second partner at the time, gifted me books by his favourite author, we started talking a lot about short stories and I shared with him ideas I had for my high fantasy novel. I told him about the *Elves*, the *Ice Forest* and the *Glacier of a Thousand Tears*. He said, "*Palace of a Thousand Tears* would be way better! No, wait, *Desert of a Thousand Regrets*!" At first, I was vexed. How could he not appreciate the epic names I'd created! But then he continued, "And there would be scarabs coming to collect the tears of people. No, even better, crystallised regrets! Grains of sand that the beetles would carry away, to free the poor souls from their sadness! Take each and every single one of them into the *Desert of a Thousand Regrets*." I was blown away. It was good. I wrote it down and told him I would work on it as soon as I had time and inspiration. I needed to wait for the story to come to me, to shape itself in my head. When Caio left New Zealand to return to his home country of Brazil, I knew it was time, and the words came out as a poem.

# 8
# THE WHISPERING WOODS

This story is the result of a *Dungeon and Dragon* one-shot that I had created for my friends. One of their characters, Kinglsey, had a powerful background story that I decided to include in the storytelling of the game. The session turned out to be a huge success and everyone got spooked and creeped out by the Ectoplasm and Georgia. I then decided to write down the *Whispering Woods* to include all the elements I could not include in the game (as all DM know the frustration). It took me ages to give birth to the final draft, but I am happy with the result. I just hope you won't regret reading it.

# 1
# KIM AND LEE

Kim was upset. She was walking in circles with all her muscles tensed under her caramel skin. As usual, Lee had forgotten about the bus schedule and, once again, they were trapped in the wopwops: Turakina. She rolled her eyes to the sky when she saw her partner sit down and open his book. How could he stay so calm when she was on the verge of a panic attack! She bit her lower lip out of frustration, and the wind blew through her loose auburn braid, making her shiver a little.

Lee's blond, curly hair was all tangled by the light breeze. His thin, pale fingers caressed the book while reading, as if the object was a beloved cat purring in his hands. He had no idea about the trouble stirring his girlfriend's mind. All that mattered was the story, the plot, wizards, elves and dragons.

Kim shot a rock on the road, but the noise did not even disturb Lee's inner peace. Helpless, she sat down next to him and instantly felt relaxed by the touch of the soft, fresh grass on her bare skin. She looked at Lee — how he would whisper some of the words he read with that intense look he has when he is hooked on the story — and realised that she could play the guitar to feel the same way. She hastily opened the leather case laid next to her and revealed its treasure. Kim put her palm on the metal strings and enjoyed their cold pressure. She then stroked the shiny wooden body, rediscovering the curves of her instrument. As she played the first chord, Lee shouted, "Thunder!" and suddenly, a lightning bolt ripped the sky apart in a tremendous sound.

Lee stared at the ink trickling, thunderstruck, as the rain droplets fell onto his favourite book.

"What the heck just happened, love?"

Kim opened her mouth, speechless, and plucked a string. Nothing.

Already, their belongings were soaked by the inexplicable shower. Two seconds ago, the sun was bright in a clear blue sky, and, after an unexpected blinding flash, the air was now charged with electricity!

Kim played another chord, in vain. An earthy taste filled her mouth when the water seeped in through her lips. Her partner was desperately examining his book from every angle. One wet page stayed between his fingers as he was trying to unglue it from another one. The piece of paper had imprinted words on his thumb. Lee tried to decrypt the blurry scribble.

"Boat?"

The melodic sound of Kim's guitar gave harmony to his question, and a little paper boat sneaked out from behind the bushes, floating cheekily on a swirling, recently formed puddle.

They both gawked at the origami canoe, agog. When a frog leaped into the water with a splashy noise, a wave of muddy water rose and challenged the tiny boat's balance. But as the minute tsunami was about to hit its white hull, the vessel started to grow. Bigger and bigger, the boat was now as big as a car! Kim and Lee, petrified, saw the frog jump from the now two-meter-high paper deck and swim away to find shelter in the grass.

"Incredible!"

Kim stroked the rough surface of the paper. How could the boat feel so robust yet fragile? The storm had eased off, only a small breeze was cooling the air. Out of her mind, Kim grabbed the edge of the hull and dragged herself onto the deck. The vessel was surprisingly totally watertight.

"You should join, love!", she said.

Lee seemed to be trapped in a state of extreme astonishment. His girlfriend played a discordant chord to get him out of his reverie. He instantly regained consciousness, as if the fog had lifted from his mind.

"Hop on, come on!"

Obeying like a muppet, Lee pulled himself up. He could not take off his hands from the paper guardrail, reassured to feel the tangibility of this magical boat. In the background, the smooth sound of the guitar filled the silence. He let himself swing to the melody. Each note, each chord, each pause, were another step deep in this dream. He imagined the boat moving, the paper sails filled by the wind, Palmy on the horizon.

A loud gasp echoed. The music stopped. Lee opened his eyes to see the waters rising and their skiff floating on the flooded highway.

"I don't want this dream to stop.", he whispered to himself.

Kim was now showing off her skills as a musician. Rhythm, unexpected harmony, she was creating something unique. The craft followed the instructions, zigzagged off the road in between fences and trees, guided by the magical sound of the enchanted guitar.

In the meantime, Lee devoured with his wide-opened eyes the familiar yet different landscape of his hometown, fading as they sailed away. Time passed slowly and, without them noticing, their journey came to an end. As the sun set, Kim and Lee arrived in Palmerston North. They got off the boat, expecting their feet to sink in the water. Instead, a soft, grassy bed cushioned their landing. They turned around, panicked. The origami vessel was gone, vanished!

A shiny tear rolled down Kim's cheek. Lee grabbed her hand, pulled her to him and kissed the salty droplet off. A toad croaked in the distance. They both giggled and cuddled tightly, eyes closed, embracing their love.

Three feet away, in the Town Square's pond, a tiny paper boat was floating away with a green slimy toad as its only passenger.

# 2
# TIME IS PASSING

Time is passing—such an obvious statement and yet difficult to grasp when you are caught up in your life. Of course, you know you're getting old: your bones are cracking, your back is sore, and you can't handle a hangover any more. You reflect on your past self while drinking your chamomile tea at six o'clock, right before your bedtime, because you need your ten hours of sleep. You wonder how you ended up like this: comfy slippers, a blanket on your lap and being grumpy at the kids loudly playing outside. So, in a vain attempt to prove yourself that you're still young, and that you've still got it, you jump in the shower, dress up and hit town. You have put on your high heels, red lipstick and smoky eyeshadow, and this dress that you bought ages ago, thinking you would look cute, but you just look like you're wearing a costume to fit in with the teens lining up in front of the bar.

"Ma'am," someone says in the crowd, and you laugh at this poor soul, already old and crusty-looking, to be called like that. But it's you. It's you this kid is talking to. The youth of his skin, seasoned with acne scars and sweat, reminds you that this whole trip was absurd, you don't belong here. You are not even strong enough to reply; you just flee, scared to face the truth: time has been passing.

On your way back home, you look around, gaze at the streets that saw you grow up and become the person you are today. You stop in front of that fountain where you had your first kiss, touch the stone where you painted your initials with nail polish, but wait… it's gone. The granite is smoothly cleaned, no graffiti. Time is passing, and you're only starting to realise it.

The panic fills your lungs; your breath is short, and your heart is racing. You crunch as the pain in your stomach terrifies you. Was anything else changed before your blinded eyes? You sit down at the same spot where, as a thirteen-year-old, you first tasted the strawberry ChapStick of the prettiest girl you had ever laid your eyes on. You do remember the smell of her hair: honey, coconut and argan oil. This memory is imprinted in your brain, burnt in your flesh by your flaming love. It is so clear in your head that you can smell it in the night breeze. You close your eyes and dive into this ocean of emotions that you thought were gone, buried deep in the grave of a romance that never bloomed. The smooth lips, the soft cheek, the smiley eyes. She was absolutely gorgeous. Like a marionette, you lift your hand and pass your fingers through her imaginary silky black locks, playing with one of them, bouncing it on your palm. She laughs, and your whole soul flies up in the sky like dandelion seeds, carried higher, closer to heaven, her voice like a carillon of happiness.

"Ma'am."

You snap back to reality: it's the kid from the club. He came to apologise. But then the strangest words came out of his mouth.

"I know it's probably not the case, but I'm pretty sure you know my mom."

So, you look at him, and it hits you like a wave. The curve of the face, the half-smile and the curls. The wind lifts some of his hair and you are back down memory lane as honey, coconut and argan oil scents make you suffocate on missed opportunities.

You are about to collapse, but you are already seated, so you just croak like a frog. He looks at you, intrigued but kindly. You don't hear a word he says, and he is now next to you, smiling from ear to ear, happy as she was when you confessed your love. Why? Why now? Time was passing.

You stand up, ignoring his calls. Your body knows the way home, and you have no strength to deal with the pain anyway. Only thirteen, and yet the hate and bullying made you grow up so fast. "Disgusting", "pussy-eating devil," all those nasty names you've been called. You suffered, but you grew stronger. Have you though? No. You just grew blinder and numbed. You've repressed joy, love and attraction because they were so intertwined with ire, hurt and sorrow. One could think that teenage love is childish, short-lived and fast-burning, but you've never got the opportunity to properly live it. One day she was kissing you, and the next day she was gone. She left you with an aching heart that you knew would never heal. You fell into a darkness that you created, a cage you locked yourself in. The door could be opened, and you had the key, but why leave? Sure, it was cold, lonely and sad, but it was safe. Safe from insults and rejection. Safe from the hits and kicks. Safe from the bruises and cuts. The floor was paved with your blood that you drew from your own veins to prove yourself that you still felt something-even if it was just pain. You grew old, yes, but you grew weak. Time passed.

When you finally wake up from your trance, it is not your house that you stand in front of. Those are not your windows; this is not your garden. You don't even remember the last time you'd gardened. Your yard is full of weeds and thorns, but the one in front of you is colourful, even that late in the night. The moon is timidly shining through the clouds, and the rosemary flowers smell like Sunday roast. The gate has this beautiful shade of green, same as her eyes. You shake your head. It's enough! But you recognise this gate, you suddenly realise that you know that garden and that you smelled that rosemary bush before, in another life, a century ago, when you were thirteen. Time is a cruel thing, and so is fate. She is waving at you through the window, this ghost of your past, the beautiful poltergeist that you tried so hard to forget. Does she still have the smooth lips, the soft cheeks and the smiley eyes? For all you know, she could just be a dream, a twisted nightmare that your sick brain tattooed on your pupils, so you continue to regret nothing that happened between you two. The door opens, and she is there, in the flesh, smiling at you like time hasn't passed.

She walks towards you, opens the green gate and takes your hand. Without resisting, you follow her inside her home—this house that you once knew. Her husband is on the couch, reading, turning pages like she has with you. Tears roll from your eyes; you just can't hold them any longer. You're on the verge of fainting, legs shaking, palms sweating. You see yourself collapse on the floor, from outside your body, a silent, invisible witness of this bizarre night. She is at your side, and he is too. She is wailing, barely any wrinkles on her gorgeous face, even after all these years. She holds you closer, and you feel her heart beating as fast as yours when you kissed her that day. The warmth of her embrace is soothing. Your vampiric, soul-sucking shell feeds on her essence. You don't want to hurt her like she hurt you, but it is so nice to be held. And then you're whooshed back inside your body in an instant. Her lips are on yours, her tears flooding your neck. Her husband is holding her as she is holding you. You can hear him humming a soft song when she kisses you with such despair. It is as if you breathed for the first time, the darkness suddenly lifted. You open your eyes. She looks back at you, her sweet strawberry mouth still pressed against yours, and she laughs. The carillon of happiness echoes once again in your heart, and you laugh, and you cry more, and she cries more, but of joy now.

"I have missed you so much!"

You know you are home now; they have welcomed you into their lives. You can finally let yourself live, and by their side, time will pass.

# 3
# MICAIAH

In your eyes I see love
In my heart I am scared
How can I get rid of
This fear and be bared?

Your affection is evident
You seem so confident
And I wish I could be
As assertive and carefree.

I am enamoured with you,
your soul, your smile, your arms
Please let me be part of you,
As imperfect as I am.

In my hand only one card,
And on it I bet my scores
With this ace of hearts,
I will make mine yours.

Mica, you are my lover and friend,
My past, present and end
Take my hand and feel my soul
Be mine and take me all.

# 4
# I AM BROKEN

I thought I was the one
I thought that you needed me
But all I was really doing
Was blocking your wings
Making you believe you could not fly.

I am what's holding you down
And my never-satisfied selfishness
Is just hiding what's deep inside
I am broken
I am broken and I am too weak to fix myself
I am broken and the only way for me to ignore it
Is to try fixing someone else.

But you need no fixing
You're perfect as you are
And I am no good
I have become what I feared
Too afraid to lose, I have to control everything
There is no other way than my way
This is not a life you want to have
You are no child and I keep on making you think you are one
That you cannot achieve anything if I am not part of it

That's my darkness, and I know it has the power to destroy all the good things I have.

This little voice in my head keeps telling me to quit
To go back to where I cannot hurt anyone
And I am trying so hard not to listen to it
I am broken, and you are the only one that made me forget about it
And now that I'm away, now that all I do is destruction, this little voice is getting stronger
This little voice is pointing fingers at me
"Guilty," it says
And I want to crawl under rocks
Dive into the abyss where silence is king
Where this little voice would stop
But it's still there
Following me
Waiting at every corner.

Why would you want such a curse?
I am broken, and I don't know if it could be fixed
The only thing that I know is the genuine love I have for you
I am cherishing it, so scared to lose it
I have your heart in my chest, and I haven't been a good keeper so far
It feels like my ribs are holding it captive
Making it bleed at every pulse
And I would break my bones one by one to set it free.
If you were to ask to have it back
I'd give you what's left of it, but you could keep mine
I'd have no use of it

And I'd walk to the emptiness where I belong
Seeing my sunshine getting stronger every day now that the clouds are gone.

# 5
# MR LYCHEE

For Cameron, a beautiful soul.
— Claire

Mr Walnut was tall, strong and assertive. His demeanour would fill the room as soon as he would enter. Mr Lychee knew him but only vaguely, from the odd occasion when they would hang out with their common friends. He had been invited to a party hosted by Mr Walnut and Mx Peach, that he knew even less, hence his presence here, in the living room of their little cottage. Coming straight after work, he had been the first to arrive and he was now awkwardly sitting on the couch. Mx Peach had tried to chat with him, but his interest in small talk was as big as a pip. They had offered him a cup of juice and were waiting for the other guests to arrive.

The door opened; the cold air of this winter evening entered with Mr Walnut. Mr Lychee saw the man coming home to his wife, who instantly jumped in his arms. Mx Peach was glowing, and a sudden wave of heat flooded the room, hunting the snowflakes that were already melting anyway. To Mr Lychee's absolute astonishment, Walnut removed his coat—this hard shell that appeared to be unbreakable—and gave it to Mx Peach. They held the garment for a second, bathing in his scent, and put it away on the coat hanger, next to empty hooks.

"Welcome home, love," they said in their soft voice.

A tsunami of people arrived soon after, along with a carnival of fruits of various shapes and colours. Very few hung their coats and most of the hooks remained empty, except for Mr Walnut's. At some point, Mr Lychee thought he had seen a glimpse of a veil on one of the hangers, but Mr Kiwi's laughter snapped him back to reality. It was his turn to play.

"Fast game, good game!" shouted one guest.

After more losses than victories, the evening came to an end for Mr Lychee. He said goodbye and thanked the hosts. Mx Peach was lovingly embracing Mr Kiwi, her husband behind them, patting both their heads with a tender smile.

*What an odd bunch*, Mr Lychee thought.

When he finally arrived home, he sat on his bed and looked in the mirror. His reflection looked back at him with a smirk. Everybody tonight saw him as a suave, mysterious man, wearing this amazing spiky coat, full of colours and shining like a thousand suns. He mesmerised the audience with his deep voice and charmed them all, one by one. Not one did see a crack in his mask, a glitch in his masquerade. His performance was perfection. He had worked hard to polish every barb of his coat so they wouldn't even need light to dazzle anyone who would look at them. The trick was to never let anyone approach close enough to see how much of a hoax it all was, and so he did, for years. He only allowed a couple of trusted friends and partners to see his true self, but even so, it was hard for him not to nourish their flesh rather than tend to his own. That night, he went to bed with his coat, piercing the bed with razor-sharp thorns that used to be blunt.

Days, weeks and months passed. Mr Lychee got to know Mx

Peach better, so much so that he let down some of his guard and allowed himself to feel attraction for their velvety skin and solar smile.

One night, he opened his mouth like a mute fish, trying to spit out the poison that had been saturating his veins for so long now.

"Peach, I am no good. I don't even know who I am, what I want or what's out there for me. I'm not a lychee; I'm a leech. That's what I am. I feed on others' happiness, eager to please so I can sustain my insatiable hunger. Look at the spikes on my coat; what else could they be for? They pierce the skin of anyone who comes near, so I can transfuse my vital force into them. But when I come home and remove the coat, I'm diminished, rotten and dry. I have nothing left to give and nothing left for me."

"Then remove the coat and let other people feed you with their love!"

They said that with such ease that it could have been sarcasm. The sincerity of their gaze proved him otherwise.

*They must be insane*, he thought.

"If I do that, all will see how feeble I am, how vulnerable, how pathetic. They will mock my scars and wounds, point out my mistakes and insecurities. I couldn't suffer the burn of their fiery, vicious tongues sizzling my skin until 'failure' was written all over it."

"What kind of assholes have you met in your life?" They asked, shocked and angry at the world. "Look at me! I'm perfectly fine, and I have scars too! Yes, I've met bad people, and they hurt me. Life hurt me. But that doesn't mean life isn't beautiful or that I should hide these parts of me. I'm empowered by my weaknesses because they push me to be better, to improve day after day. And when I see wounds oozing, I clean them, stitch them, until they become pieces of art, stories to tell. They are no less part of me than my heart is."

Mr Lychee remained silent, not sure what to say next. He didn't see any scars on their skin.

"But you're not wearing a coat, are you?"

"Of course, I'm wearing a coat! You're just too blind to see it, silly."

In a beam of sun, Mr Lychee saw the vest for the first time indeed. It was a translucent, shimmering veil, so thin that he could see Peach's skin as clear as if they were naked. But he could see no scars, no bruises, no blemishes. They smiled, and his heart fluttered, lifting the coat for an instant as Peach was lovingly looking at his face. Then he saw, briefly but clearly, that their heart was beaten up and patched with a million stitches. He looked away, as if not allowed the sight of their vulnerability.

"Look," they said, "that's from the first time we met." They showed him punctures in their flesh, already healing, oddly symmetrical, somehow decorating their thorax like a tattoo. "I cherish them and will continue to, as they remind me of the wonderful person you are. I am grateful to have met you, and you left your trace on the tapestry of my skin. Let me show you more."

With their delicate hands, they unfastened their coat. They looked deeply into his eyes until he felt himself drowning in their very essence. This intimacy was almost burning his soul; he could even smell it in the air, feral yet irresistible. The sight of Peach revealing themselves was just breath-taking. He had seen them naked before, but this time it felt different. They were glowing, pulsing with life, and filled with vital energy like a supernova. Their soul was hot magma swirling underneath a paper-thin and fragile skin covered in marks. They took his hand

and placed it on a cut. Out of fear of somehow hurting Peach, he resisted the urge to touch any of their other wounds. At last, he gave in and felt the warmth of the rough patches on their otherwise silky skin. His eyes opened widely, stunned that scars could be what made one unique and beautiful.

Without a thought, he let Peach open his vest, one button at a time. The heat on his flesh, almost unbearable but somehow soothing, reminded his body of sensory delights he forgot existed. Empathetic, smooth fingers caressed his flesh, and shivers ran down his back, electric, revivifying. His shoulders, free from any protection, tightened under the affectionate touch. He knew damn well the scars that carved his body from all the self-flagellation, all the years of beating himself up for mistakes he had done, roads he had left, choices he had made. Shame and guilt froze the air as icy serpents grasped his guts. His shallow breath deprived his brain from oxygen, nurturing the panic that boiled deep in his cells.

"What a masterpiece!" they said.

His heart skipped a beat. Warm hands were following the hills and valleys of his damaged back, travelling on a territory they discovered for the first time, taking paths he had forgotten. Tears rolled down his face, carving small rivers on his cheeks.

The spiky coat was now on the floor. Naked, vulnerable, Mr Lychee no longer feared to show his flesh to Peach. The oozing wounds were part of him, and he had to let them heal. His own warmth joined Peach's in an aerial dance that wiped clean his cuts, like a tornado removing black oil from the surface of the ocean. For once, he was at peace with himself, his body engorged with life once again.

They spent hours together, telling stories of loving and being loved. With Peach in his arms, he looked at the mirror: two partners, naked, glistening from the love they shared; and he smiled.

"Are you happy to have met the person you should have loved all this time?" they asked.

"You?"

They laughed, genuinely taken by surprise.

"No, silly! Yourself!"

# 6
# FLESH AND STONE

**1. THE FOUR OF YOU**
The blood moon has been shining for a month now. You've been out hunting for about the same time. The jungle, usually filled with life, has been silent as a tomb. After a week, you found a dead jaguar left untouched by decomposition, and you managed to scavenge enough food to sustain your party. The meat was tough and somehow tasted like ashes. You didn't think much of it. Until today.

You heard them in the night, howling, crying, and eating. The sound of the tribe under attack will forever stay imprinted in your memory, the blood of families staining the inside of your eyelids like a macabre painting. You saw limbs piled up in front of the main temple, dripping red all over the cobblestone. You recognised some of the decapitated heads, even as disfigured as they were: the shaman, your neighbour's son, and the healer. All dead.

You heard someone sobbing. As you approached, you saw an unknown girl, war paint on her face, holding an open adult ribcage, rocking back and forth. Her sorrow was so powerful that you couldn't bear to look at her much longer. You cried and closed your eyes, wishing this was all a dream. The child's sobbing stopped. When you opened your eyes, the upper half of the little girl was gone; her legs cut clean, lying next to the body she was holding.

They are still here, watching; you can feel it on your skin. Being the hunter for so long, you forgot how it felt to be the prey. It would be wise to go to the temple or the nearby tribe, but your soul wants to venture into the heart of the jungle to fight them and get your revenge.

## 2. HURARI

"Where is my husband? Where is my son?"

You don't recognise your voice. It sounds like a croak. You kneel in front of your *teyoupa,* or what's left of it. Your hut is a mix of ashes and flesh, with the skin of the walls still pulsing from an evil life that you've never seen before. The door is just a wound now, oozing blood and... what looks like human limbs fused together at odd angles. Queasy is how you feel, hearing the wound door giving birth to this gore.

Next to you, your hunting party is in shock: Paris is puking, Ameiwa silently crying and Sawayu already coming back to her senses.

"Hurari, we need to go. They are coming. Nothing can be done. Let's go!"

The scout leaves you to your grief, swiftly walking towards the temple.

You observe the *Tusawa*'s son, his face wet as a river. It was his first hunt, the ritual to become an adult. The boy is strong, prepared to be the next chief ever since he was able to walk, but this is too much, even for you and your moons of experience. The child presses the head of the *Tusawa* against his chest, petting the hair of his mother as if she were still alive. Her spine rattles against the blades attached to his belt, even though no wind is to be felt. The Chief being dead, he is now next in line.

Standing close to him, Paris, the British botanist and anthropologist that your tribe rescued from the jungle. You don't like him, nobody does, but he had been incredibly helpful recently, writing down your people's history using symbols he called letters. Amongst the things he brought from his home island: pen, ink and paper; a sharp stick, dark liquid; and wet pressed wood pulp dried to be used as canvas. His Queen asked him to draw whatever the jungle had to offer: plants, animals, fungi and minerals. On his own initiative, he also decided to write about your people, their language and myths too. He joined the hunt against your will. The *Tusawa* told you that he was not your responsibility, and if he happened to die, nobody would mourn a *karaiba*. Several times you thought about feeding him to the jungle, but you remembered he helped your husband when the healer couldn't. Now, you glance at him with pity: the poor white man is so pale he almost looks like *sharinga* sap. His vomit mixes with the blood on the floor, and he barfs once more.

"Hurari! Come!"

Sawayu is at the top of the temple stairs. She sounds worried and impatient. With a nod, you order your party to follow you. The boy and the outsider move like undead muppets, as if the gods controlled their legs and brain. Without a look back, you climb up the high stone steps. Your lungs cry, and your breath is short. Finally, you're next to your scout.

"What is it? What have you found?"

Without a word, she points at the altar.

You let out a cry so loud that every atom around you vibrates with your rage. The small body already smells like rotten flesh, and flies buzz around what used to be your son.

## 3. SAWAYU

Hurari's metamorphosis amazes you. You haven't been blessed by the blood moon like he was, and in a sense, you are grateful. The cracking of bones, the tears of muscles—everything is just sickening. From what you've been told, wolf-borns still feel the pain of their bodies rearranging themselves, every cell bursting out of its human form to reshape how the moon dictates.

The claws and fangs as big as your hand, Hurari is now as large as the door. The gigantic shoulders, thickly covered with green-grey fur, block the red light from outside. In this semi-darkness, you know they could attack unseen.

"Hurari, take him, we need to go."

The wolf can't speak but understands you. With a soft bite, he cups the baby in between his jaws. Blood drips as he moves towards the exit on his four legs. The clicks of his claws make you shiver, and you know not to linger: innocent blood has been spilled on sacred stones. You look up to the opening in the ceiling. A cloud covers the moon, and you hear them howl.

On your way out, you murmur a prayer to the Gods, one never knows when divine aid will be needed. From the terrace, the village looks like burnt-out carnage. Nothing moves but the silhouettes of your party: you, two of your kind and a *karaíba*, not much hope to defeat them. The canopy moves up and down; only evil thrives when the jungle breathes.

From what you remember, the Urubu tribe could help. Sure, alliances faded with time, but it is your only chance. The road would be long and dangerous, especially with the white weakling. On the horizon, you can barely see the summit of their temple. Let's hope their blood has been spared. In a few jumps, you are next to your party.

"Oh, my sweet Lord, what is that monster?"

Paris always rubs you the wrong way. His high-pitch voice pierces your over-sensitive eardrums. You had forgotten his ignorance. Seeing a wolf-born for the first time can break a spirit. The muzzle, as bulky as a grown man's chest, could snap a body like a branch. The eyes, flaming green spirals, could suck your soul out of your flesh if stared at for too long. What not to fear? For once, you sympathise with the poor man.

"Friends, we need to head east. Let's join the Urubu before the plague gets there. Ameiwa, Chief, please, give the order."

The sweat drips from the tip of your black hair. The heat and humidity are what you are used to, and yet a breeze as cold as Death dries the wetness on your neck. In the night, the ginger-brown of your skin is the best camouflage: you are Sawayu, Red Monkey, the best scout of the tribe. However, the decision is not yours.

"East, we go."

Ameiwa, still holding the butchered skull of your *Tusawa*, walks towards the road swallowed by the jungle and its darkness. Hurari sniffs the air and looks west. The river road was the second option, the one you would have chosen if you felt there had been a chance to win. Glancing over the remains of your tribe, your blood boils. Revenge will be done, a promise whispered in the night to all those dead witnesses.

You catch up with Ameiwa and Paris, already so close to the dark mouth of the jungle. Hurari could join the party later. Giving an only son to the river is to be done alone, sorrow must be borne in solitude.

Back in your scouting position, several jumps ahead of your group, the jungle eats you and traps you in its leafy throat. You follow the bushy entrails, venturing deep into the humid, wooden bowels of the forest. No chirp, no cry, only silence and the mayhem of your scared crew trying to be discreet: they are prey, easy targets to be digested by the vegetal intestines. You keep going, relieved that predators have deserted the trail, taken by the plague.

## 4. AMEIWA
You are the chief now.

The mouth of your dead mother will never tell you what to do any more. You could run; you could go to that paradise island where Paris comes from and experience life in a cottage, eating roasted lamb and garlic bread. You are free.

You are the chief now.

Bloody lips move in the dark, a nightmare on a still face. You should have gone with Hurari and fed the *Tusawa* to the river like the common folk do. Your mother's head, attached to your belt by the braids, would probably sink with the weight of her stubbornness. You smile at the thought.

You are the chief now.

Her exposed vertebra slither like a boa's skeleton, and you wouldn't be surprised if her jaws unhinged to swallow your arrogant dream. Is her skull alive? Maybe her spirit is still trapped, waiting for you to liberate it from earthly bonds through sacred fire. Your *angûera* roams within you, ready to take control. Maybe he could be *Tusawa*. What a life it would be, cosy in the spirit world while your inner creature acts on your behalf.

"Chief, we should stop for the night. We have covered enough ground. The Urubu territories are close enough."

Damn, Red Monkey, you had forgotten about her. Surely, she would force you to take on your birthright and rise as the tribe chief. Your party sets up camp and falls asleep with Paris' sobs as a lullaby.

In the morning, the dew is thick and red, tears of the blood moon like in the legends. Already, Sawayu gathers her weapons and shakes Paris out of his sleeping torpor. The blond-orange hair of the outsider stands out in the dim light. Without a word, you continue your journey.

After half a day of tramping, the clearing is visible in the distance. On your way there, rays of light pierce the canopy like a thousand mortal arrows before you reach the village. The temple, bigger than the Wolf-Stone, sits in the centre of the assembly of *teyoupa*. Jewels are embedded within the wall of the Bird-Stone, decorating the Urubu temple with various colours. What a sight!

The welcoming crew paces towards you, all covered in rainbow feathers, dancing and chanting in a language familiar in meaning but foreign in sound. Their calls are joyful and unthreatening, very different from Sawayu's answer. Her howling tears echo the gay melody of the ritual, announcing death and sorrow.

The bird people retreat swiftly, their foreheads so close to the earth that worms could probably eat their eyelashes. Red Monkey steps back and intimates Paris to do the same. You are left alone, and you know what to do.

You are the chief now.

## 5. PARIS

Your life amongst the savages has been tougher than you expected. Every day, you have prayed the Lord to come to your rescue, holding the Union Jack in your sweaty palms, but you have been left unanswered. Sure, the natives have shown you so much and taught you knowledge that a whole library couldn't contain, but still, the Red-Faces scare your very soul.

They dressed you like them and removed your clothes that used to cover your dignity. You got used to the leathery skirt around your waist, but not to the feeling of the air tickling your groin as you walked. Your bare chest, white as their teeth, is now covered in scars from that evil jungle you lost yourself in nine years ago. Nobody here has hair like yours, nobody here understands your language, you are alone.

When Hurari saved you from certain death, you thought of him as the devil. His glistening muscles, so tough compared to your bony chest, triggered a desire you had refrained from for so long. That night, you lashed your back with the thorny vine that grows around most of the trees here. The pain relieved you of the desire, and you asked for another leathery skirt.

Nights in the tribe are dreadful: weird noise, moist whizz, everything that you hate, and this constant heat and muggy climate would probably kill you faster than a jaguar. For years, you have drawn plants so strange they could be Satan's seeds, seen animals so odd you couldn't sleep for months and eaten fungi so delicious you floated amongst angels for three days. And yet, nothing would have prepared you for dire wolves.

Hurari, ferocious canine, bigger than an ox, holding his baby boy in his sharp-tooth mouth, you almost felt sicker than after seeing the massacre of blood and ashes. You remembered healing his intersex husband after he had given birth, bleeding like a slaughtered pig. The baby was beautiful, the fruit of their love. The jealousy had burned your veins, and for the first time, you had hated your home, the Queen and your religion. For the first time, you wanted to be one of them.

You know they tolerate you, but they do not like you, your judgement or your Bible. The Holy Words are of no use to them, and the sins you'd been taught as a child have no meaning here, so you stopped preaching. Your faith shape-shifted; from unbreakable laws of life to guidelines for community and personal fulfilment. You took a lover, or rather, a lover took you, and doused the fire of shame your Church had fuelled for so long. He was dead now, half cut and rotting amongst the other villagers. Now you followed them to the Urubu settlement. There was no point in your staying behind.

Before your *karaíba* eyes, they perform a ritual: the hosts are dancing like birds, welcoming you, into their village and its safety. The scout approaches the welcoming crew and wails. The scream grasps your heart and soul; it's a howl of death and grief. The birds step back, and you get a hint from the scout that you should do the same. You don't really understand until the boy—sorry, the chief—starts to change.

You are unfamiliar with shapeshifters, but the iconography of the temple that they call Wolf-Stone made it obvious with which animal the tribe was connected. You gasp when blue scales cover the skin of the child. A drake! His name makes sense now: Blue Lizard, an animal that you never spotted in the jungle. But why? Aren't they supposed to be werewolves? You ask yourself rational questions as if the whole situation were not already surreal.

The Urubu chief approaches, naked and old, wrinkled from

head to toe. Her breast is muscly and almost flat; her stomach stilled scarred from an open-womb birth; and her sex is a mix between male and female. She comes to the drake-boy and places her forehead on its temple. Scales start covering her cheeks, skull and back, green as fresh leaves.

Her wyvern form is bird-like: two back legs and a pair of wings; talons like razors; a beak as sharp as a harpoon. The wolf-drake, wingless and bulky, lowers his head in submission. She inhales, sucking in the heat and humidity of the air surrounding her. Her chest starts glowing like an inferno, with green swirls and white sparks visible through her tough skin. The blue drake closes his black eyes and opens his jaws beneath hers.

In the silence of the jungle, the fire breath blasts like thunder, from beak to muzzle, created by one and swallowed by the other. Green flames burn the oxygen, and your lungs start to struggle, your vision blurs and you are on the verge of collapsing. All the Red-Faces are humming, using air that you would desperately breathe. Their chanting gets louder, louder than the supranatural blaze, until silence strikes again in a snapping sound of fangs.

### 6. AMEIWA

You feel her fire in you, her knowledge and the history of your land and ancestors. Your mother couldn't perform the ritual herself, and you are unsure what to expect. The Urubu *Tusawa* is a wyvern; you are a drake as blue as she is green. You swallowed her inferno, and your body did the rest. The *caraba* boils in your fire chamber, ready to burn like *sharinga* sap. Now you can face them and defeat the plague. You open your eyes and see the old lady, human and fragile, smiling at you like your mother never did.

All kneel in front of you. Hitting the earth with their fists, they remind you of your beating heart. A growl forms in your throat, and the *caraba* fills up your flame chamber. In an instant, the sacred oil ignites in a magnificent water blue blaze that you expel from your open mouth. The flame hits the Urubu *Tusawa* and a nearby *teyoupa*. The woman dances in the fire, surrounded by the ashes of the house you've just burned down.

Your drake form resorbs. Under the blood moon, your skin looks even redder than usual. You feel drained, but you know you should head back before the Wolf-Stone starts moving.

## 7. SAWAYU

Beautiful. You are lost for words. The ritual went well—better than expected. It was unheard of that *angûera* from different tribes could awaken each other, but the Gods may have had mercy. Ecstatic, your fist pounds the ground with your siblings as you witness the birth of your *Tusawa*. If the First Hunt makes one an adult, the *Caraba* Communion turns potential into reality. You are proud. Next to you, Paris struggles to breathe, especially when the blue fire breath burns the hut close to him. When the ritual is done, the poor man is covered in ashes, his face smudged with tears and sweat. For once, he is quiet, even though his mouth is wide open.

Now that your *Tusawa* has risen, you must be on your way to find Hurari and defeat the Wolf-Stone to free it from the plague. Hope has returned! You smile.

Suddenly, the ground breaks open, tearing the earth beneath your feet. Some Urubu people fall into the abyss; Paris is holding on to the edge, screaming like a new-born, and you are in the air, flying, rescued from certain death by friendly talons still holding you in their grasp. The green wyvern puts you down next to your chief and takes off to face the Bird-Stone. The temple frees its legs from the ground in a rain of jewels and stomps multiple *teyoupa* in its clumsy awakening. So, the plague had stroked it too…

You help Paris, give him one of your weapons, and point at the moving building. The temple unhinges its hidden limbs from its side, waving them in the air, trying to fly. The stone wings, after aeons of immobility, create a wave of wind that hits you with the strength and weight of an attacking jaguar. The building doesn't leave the ground much before landing in an earthquake that widens the deathly fault even more.

In the air, the green wyvern streaks the sky with emerald fire arrows, hitting the Bird-Stone without visible effects. On the ground, the blue drake runs, gains momentum and launches himself onto the stone steps of the temple. His fire is timid but amplifies as he climbs up the stairs, towards the heart of the building, burning the rocky surface already free of its decorative jewels.

You know the altar should be burned, cleansed from the plague by sacred burning *caraba*. Only then the temple would settle down and the horror would end. You trust Ameiwa.

## 8. PARIS
As the Bird-Stone's legs puncture the ground with its stone talons, its wings flap and hit the canopy in a racket of broken wood. Behind you, coming from the west, a distant din resonates in the dead jungle. Ashes fill the air as the Wolf-Stone jumps and lands on the other moving temple. The fracas of rocks covers the tumult of the fight. Blocks crash close to you in deep craters: a canine-shaped building strikes the winged temple with its massive stone paw, leaving a hole in the structure.

Dust, ash and leaves float in the air, making it hard for you to see what's happening in this monochrome scene. Only three flashes of colours attract your attention: red, round and full, the blood moon shines through the clouds; green, rapid and slick, the wyvern deflects attacks with elegance; and blue, powerful and precise, the drake strikes relentlessly, hoping to breach the sealed door and access the altar.

You don't understand; why would the other temple—the wolf one—assault the Bird-Stone? You turn to ask Sawayu, but the scout is gone, running through flying rocks as if it were inoffensive rain, her blade reflecting the red light of the moon. You look at the weapon in your hand, unsure how useful it could be in this titan fight. The gargantuan buildings could crush you in so many ways; why would you even bother risking your life here? You should run, and so you do.

Your legs move as fast as they can, the muscles screaming from the pain of the sprint. The jungle used to scare you with its darkness and hidden threats; now, it is welcoming, and you can't wait to take cover under its protective branches. On your way, you notice a shape inside the altar room of the Wolf-Stone, but it could be your shocked mind playing tricks. In a leap, you land on the leafy ground and crawl out of reach of the falling rocks.

## 9. HURARI

You have returned your child to the river. You have cried and wailed, gathered strength and fuelled it with rage. In your wolf form, your senses are sharper. You hear the distant chaos that could only mean one thing: the Wolf-Stone has awakened. Sprinting towards the ruins of your village, another racket booms in the east. It is much worse than you thought.

Back in the clearing, still filled with gore, ashes and body parts, you witness your temple dislocating its block and taking its canine shape. On the brink of madness, you attempt the impossible: dashing towards the building, you then leap in the air and land on what used to be tall stone steps. The door is not yet closed, and you can still see the altar, pulsing with a fleshy evil, the result of the sacrifice of your innocent son. You cover the distance in a split second. Taking your last chance, you jerk forward as the temple tries to hit you with one of its limbs, and you land half-conscious within the altar room. In a desperate bite, you sink your poisonous fangs into the heart of your enemy.

The Wolf-Stone roar vibrates throughout its structure, and your jaws struggle to hold their grasp as the temple starts moving. Under your legs, you feel the floor, mushy and wet; the tiles are covered in flesh, and the plague expands rhythmically, in synch with the pounds of the altar-heart. You must avoid the temple to complete its transformation! With your sharp claws, you cut open the skin, revealing stone-grey veins. The Wolf-Stone jolts, and you lose grip. Perfect! Your fangs penetrate the exposed veins.

The feeling is incredible. You control the titan; its limbs and force are yours to move and use, so you make your way east. Somehow, your son is with you, and so is all your village, trapped in spirit and converted in flesh as the plague consumes stone. You draw from their energy to maintain control, guiding the temple to the fight that would end this folly. The first one to vanish is your husband. His soul suddenly evaporates, and so do the shaman's, the healer's and your son's. You grieve for them as they go, grateful for their sacrifice.

You must be in the Urubu village now, and you must temple-launch yourself into combat. The impact challenges your clutch: fourteen villagers are consumed for you to maintain command.

Your wrath turns into fury, and your poison into lava. The Wolf-Stone strikes the Urubu temple again and again. You aim at the door, as it is the only way to defeat the Bird-Stone. Through tremor sense, you realise that you are not fighting alone: something is on the surface of the bird temple, making its way up. You hope it's your *Tusawa.*

In a loud thunder, your proxy's stone claws ripped the roof of your enemy open. You seize the opportunity to temple-jump on the Bird-stone; your rocky paws grapple the wings; and you pin the titan to the ground. Your hind legs crush your foe's as your tremor-sense feels two creatures heading towards the opened summit. Your work here is done, and only a few villagers are still present with you.

**10. AMEIWA**
With no clue why the Wolf-Stone started attacking its ally, you stopped trying to understand as it provided you with opportunities to climb higher and reach the vulnerable heart. Finally, one hit destroyed the top of the Bird-Stone in a cascade of sharp gravel. Your tough scales protected you from most of the projectiles; some pierced your skin like jaguar fangs. The pain gave you speed as adrenaline filled your veins. A couple of metres, and you would be able to access the altar room. Suddenly, you lose balance, and you are projected forward as the Bird-stone is being pinned down.

At the periphery of your vision, the wyvern flies into the altar room. You gather what's left of your strength and join her for the final blow. Inside the dusty room, the fleshy, cursed altar continues to grow and consume the life of the jungle. The skin, muscle, and evil meat replace tiles and blocks of stone; the whole room is alive and organic. Each of your steps is sucked into the plague mucosa. The moist sound is so disgusting that you retch, envious of your flying ally.

Together, with talons and claws, you slice chunks of flesh, digging through tough muscles to expose the vulnerable veins. The wounds ooze plague, thick and blood-like. It magically heals the lesions faster than you inflict them. In its pain, the temple jerks and jolts, your whole world is shaken, and you struggle to keep attacking with precision. After minutes of efforts and determination, one laceration cuts deep enough to open the altar heart and reveal veins fused in an ash-grey sphere. Victory!

Connected through the magic of your people, ancient spirit-bonds sealed with time and blood, your *angûera* and the Urubu chief's fill your lungs with air, ready to scorch the evil with sacred blazing *caraba.* Heat rises as blue and green mix in darker flames, burning down the grey plague once and for all. Defeated, the Bird-Stone collapses, and its structure crumbles. The titan lies inert on the ground, still pinned down by the wolf-shaped temple, very much alive and cursed.

Without hesitation, you both make your way towards the last enemy. The task is not difficult, as if the Wolf-Stone wanted you to end this madness. The building helps you, bending its neck for easier access. The door is open, and you recognize Hurari, fangs deep in the altar's heart. Gratitude fills your soul as you and your wyvern-friend blaze the whole room to ashes.

# 7
# THE SCARABS OF TIME

You left two days ago, or was it yesterday? Time has no meaning any more. I navigate between rivers of tears and cascades of pain, each as dreadful and overwhelming as the other. I steer the boat with my feeble arms, facing whatever will come next. So far, so good. So far, so good... So far, so... Shit! You are there, in the smell of a delicious breakfast, in the melody of a song, in the rainbow among the clouds. The ship rocks in this storm of feelings that I had no clue could be so strong. And then the waters are calm again. Am I numb yet?

You told me about them: the scarabs of time, the insects of life, the beetles of wishes and regrets. They have had a lot of names, many forms and different stories, but one remains the same: they are here to help. You told me they would keep me company, they would wipe away my tears and transcend the pain. They did not. I saw them for what they really are: ugly little critters, coming at night to steal my dreams; during the day to spoil my hope. No, I do not like them, and I don't understand how they can be of any aid.

One took a beautiful memory. They ripped it from the fabric of my soul. They ripped it without hesitation, leaving the dangling threads around the hole. It was a memory of you—our first kiss, a night in your arms or a fight, I do not remember, they took it away.

Another came just before dawn and cupped a tear in their little legs. So close to my eyes, I saw their beauty: the iridescent elytra, the composed eyes, the delicate punctures on their carapace. And they vanished. Fleeting moment of ephemeral contemplation. I do not remember what I was crying about.

The last one stayed a little longer. They landed on my hand at work and opened the translucent wings with veins like lace. Nothing was as beautiful as them. They crawled up to my ear and whispered in a familiar voice, "You are ready." Was I? They did not answer, for they were gone.

When the sandman came, I allowed myself to accept his gift. I followed him where I could feel pain and regrets among all the memories that would not be created, only to discover a desert land, arid and bare. I looked at him, confused: what about you? What about our life together? Where were all of the things we lived? The ugly, gorgeous critters flew in the dark sky. I recognised three of them, and another, and another. There, the *I Love You* that was said in your sleep; here, the sadness of a month apart; right in front of me, a tapioca filled with cheese.

I started crying, thinking that what I thought I had processed was going to take me down like a gigantic tsunami. The sea rose, but only to decorate the desert with lovely islands. The rain came, but only to sculpt dunes and oasis. The storm passed and left behind a land where you and I will roam forever. The sandman smiled, and the critters chirped.

Grief and loss are hard, but time helps. I gave space for my emotions to bloom into a colourful heaven. You are not gone;

you are here with me, and I am there with you. There will be moments of doubt and instants of pain, and that sand of crystallised regrets will be crushed under a time; a pressure so strong that it will become jewels. Jewels of our eternal love.

# 8
# THE WHISPERING WOODS

*Dear love of mine,*

*I hope this letter will find you as well as I am right now, under this gorgeous summer sun. The travel was difficult and tiring, but I made it without too many blisters! Your son is quite agitated, and I think I know why:*

*Do you remember Albert, the toy maker who lost his wife after she gave birth? Well, he disappeared! Nothing is certain yet, but Georgia, the inn tenant, who would pay for juicy gossips, is telling everyone that Albert stopped coming down for his evening meal and started sending his son, Ivy, to pick it up instead. They went to their house after that to check on the old fellow, but the cottage was empty, as if nobody had lived in it for weeks! One night, they followed Ivy under the cover of the darkness. He walked into the Whispering Woods! Can you believe that? A kid, defenceless, in those haunted woods! Georgia couldn't find the courage to follow him any further, but they are now spreading rumours in town. Sure, it's good for business and for explorers in quest of some thrills and gold, but the whole story left me upset and uneasy for the future. I don't want our son to live so close to danger. What if it's one of those blood cults? Or an ancient Nightmare ready to devour anything? Love, I am scared, and I think you should come and investigate. Maybe it's nothing and I'm being overly dramatic... Please come join me at the Fluffy Fox Inn as soon as you can. I'll be waiting for you with a glass of your favourite ginger ale!*

*With all our love,*

*Lilly and Sullivan*

### 1. WHEN SWEET MOMENTS END...

After the third time reading the letter, Kinglsey still felt his guts all tangled. The beautiful handwriting of his dear wife couldn't minimise the dread of losing her and their soon-to-be babe. Dewneedin, where Lilly travelled to see her midwife cousin, was a small village, three days' walk from here, or one hard day's ride if he left at dawn. He glanced at the customers, drinking and eating, unaware of the perils he faced before opening the King's Ember. Daydreaming, or day-nightmaring, if such a word could exist, he rubbed one of his numerous scars, the only physical evidence of his dark past. To the naïve eye, it could have been any other wound on a hardworking man's skin; to him, it was a reminder that death is always closer than one thinks. The blade had cut deeply enough to trace another fate line on his palm, from his middle finger down to the wrist: self-inflicted, as all cultists do for the blood ritual. His reverie ended when the glass he was drying broke inside his clutching fist.

Nobody paid him attention; the bard continued singing about this lad rescuing his lover from an evil princess—his betrothed—and two young women were giggling, half shocked, half aroused, at the song's explicit words. Kinglsey recognised them, for he saw the two in his stables one night, discovering what fingers and mouths can do. He smiled at the irony; they were blushing at the words cock and fuck, while doing the exact same pleasures described crudely by the bard.

Next to them, the town's elder, as blind as a mole, was petting his beard in search of sweet crumbs instead of ordering a dessert. A family of four was finishing their meal in a hurry, and both parents worried about what questions their kids would ask after hearing the song. The rest of the crowd was dancing, pints in hands, spilling ale all over the floor. Among them, a young boy, eighteen years old, was glancing nervously at the bard. When the musician started the chorus, describing in great detail how to perform the act when the two lovers have cocks, he winked at the boy, who instantly reddened and sat down to hide his embarrassment under the table. Kinglsey raised his eyes to the ceiling and approached the boy. He put a key in front of him and said, "By the look of it, the stables will already be taken tonight, lad. First floor, third door on your left."

At the other table, sneaky hands were already getting under petticoats, and the girls were no longer giggling; too busy loving each other.

Kinglsey cherished this life. He felt like an ominous and invisible patron, guiding his herd towards enjoyment by providing food, drinks and a safe home for whomever was in need of a roof. When one has seen death and suffering, it feels right to witness joy. He went around the counter, grabbed the last apple pie and gave it to the elder.

"On the house, Harvey. Apple, your favourite."

The wrinkled face lit up with a toothless smile, and the old man devoured the dessert as if it were his last.

Back to his dishes, Kinglsey looked at the engraved portrait of his wife hanging across the room above the fireplace. After years of evil, raising demons from ashes, feeding sombre creatures with blood, he had found a new meaning in life, a purpose: to be the guardian of his wife's happiness and, in three weeks, their son's.

The bard finished his song under a loud clamour and applause. Kinglsey rang the last call for the remaining customers. The family had already gone, and the girls too. Harvey was still licking his plate, storing crumbs in his tangled beard. Kinglsey observed the customers leaving the inn, all smiles and laughter, full bellies, and fuller hearts. Sitting alone, the young lad was fidgeting with the key. A musician's hand grabbed his shoulder, and the couple went upstairs. Another happy night in the quiet town of Gullyend.

The room was now empty, and Kinglsey felt the weight of his worries crushing his back. If his wife was right, the life he cherished and the people he loved could be in danger. He finished cleaning the tables and mopping the floor, stacked all the glasses back on the shelves and closed the front door. With a heavy heart and a clouded mind, he went to his chambers, opened the wardrobe, pressed a hidden button and revealed a piece of his past he wished had never existed.

The blood-weapon still fit perfectly in his hands, all mighty and thirsty as it was when he used it for the last time. The ruby on the pommel glowed, and the voice spoke to him.

## 2. AND MYSTERY FILLS THE AIR…

The sun was low when Dewneedin finally appeared on the horizon. Kinglsey rode from dawn, galloping through meadows and groves, leaving his uneventful town at his back. Now, he was unsure why his wife seemed so worried: houses and shops were unchanged, roads neatly paved, and a delicious smell of roast chicken floated in the air. From all appearances, Dewneedin was, as well, the same old uneventful town it ever was.

His mare trotted to the main square, decorated in beautiful

white and yellow narcissus. The building Kinglsey was looking for stood there, all stones and ivy, with its rusty sign creaking on its hinges: The Fluffy Fox Inn. He got off the saddle, walked towards the stables and left Fern with the other horses before entering the tavern.

Opening the back door was like opening Pandora's box, but instead of all evil breaking loose, it was din, noise and racket filling the air, almost tangible and oppressing. Kinglsey was used to the hubbub but not to the mix of races present that night: dwarves, elves and humans, all chanting and dancing together; a minotaur sharing a meal with a dragonborn; even goblins entertaining the crowd by climbing on top of each other in a human-sized goblin pyramid. The performers were beautiful slither folk, with scales like gems and eyes like pearls, moving on the stage in a mesmerising dance.

Among this melting pot, Lilly was sitting in front of two glasses, one already half-empty. With her hands on her ginormous belly, she looked as beautiful as the day they'd met, five seasons ago. The white in her hair and the small wrinkles, the softness of her dreamy smile—looking at her was like falling in love again. Kinglsey walked towards his spouse when suddenly, a kizune stopped right in front of him. Their mouth opened in a toothy smirk before a growly voice spurted from behind sharp canines.

"Well, well, well, if that isn't my lovely boy, Kinglsey, in the flesh! When I saw that wife of yours the other night, I knew you would come! Are you here for the Whispering Woods or Albert's disappearance, lad? *Shh*, don't tell me just yet; let's join your waterlily."

Their fluffy paws grabbed his arm and guided him through the crowd. The inn tenant distributed smiles and flirty comments to all of their customers before sitting down in front of Lilly.

"Look what I've found, darling love; your husband, all sweaty and handsome! No wonder you have a bun in the oven!"

Kinglsey leaned down to kiss his wife's forehead, and she whispered in his ear, "As you can see, Georgia hasn't changed a bit!"

"Come on, you prude, give that woman a proper kiss, for gods' sake!"

Georgia downed a pint of black stout, burped and sniggered at the couple. For a fleeting moment, Kinglsey saw a sad veil covering their amber eyes.

He sat down next to his wife, took her hand in his and placed their palms on her round belly. They exchanged a warm and intimate glance, more eloquent than a thousand words.

"All right, all right, lovebirds. So, you know about old Albert, right? Tomorrow, I'll show you the way to his house. The kid, Ivy, he's gone too."

"What about the Whispering Woods?"

"Kinglsey, always in search of adventure I see, even after putting down that hammer of yours, aye?"

"No, that life is behind me now. Lilly, in your letter, you said the kid went into the woods and hasn't been seen ever since."

"Yes, the last time we saw him, he came to the inn and ordered a meal for his father. Then he took the food and went straight into the woods, even though the road to his house is on the opposite side of town. But Georgia can explain more than I; right, Georgia?"

The kizune seemed trapped in an unpleasant waking dream; all traces of joy had left their face. Kinglsey recognised it for what it was: guilt and remorse, or maybe the weight of the years—how old were they, anyway? Kizune didn't age like humans, but certainly not like elves either. Lilly had always talked about the inn tenant with great sympathy, sharing stories from her childhood visiting her family in Dewneedin. Georgia was particularly fond of her because Lilly studied in the capital, and on every trip, she would bring crazy tales and feed the lonely soul with extraordinary stories. From what Kingsley knew, the fox always looked like this: silvery-grey, with the voice of a lifelong pipe smoker, joyful yet intimidating. Although they didn't smell like magic, he could swear Georgia was no ordinary inn tenant. The depth of their eyes reflected wisdom and age, the sadness of someone who lost too many loved ones to time and yet still dwells on the earth in sorrow and solitude.

"Lilly, go home. There is no need to endanger your babe. I'll show Kinglsey the cottage and update him on what's going on."

The fox left the table without looking at either of them, grabbed the last call bell, and rang it. All the customers booed but knew better than to upset the old tenant. After an hour or so, the tavern was empty. Lilly kissed Kinglsey and went upstairs to her room, waved Georgia goodnight, even though the inn tenant was lost in thoughts behind the counter.

Without a word, they crossed the room and left Kinglsey alone in the dining hall, disappearing behind a door left ajar. Taking it as an invitation, the former adventurer followed them.

## 3. DIG IN THE PAST…

The room was small, filled with books and piles of papers. Georgia, seated in a chair too big for them, was preparing a pipe. The smell of dream-herb, opium and dust tickled Kinglsey's nose. He grabbed a wooden stool and sat down, waiting for them to speak. A long silence sheathed the office, as suffocating as the heavy smoke Georgia puffed. They weren't ready.

The man observed the walls, covered in portraits of women of various races, some as young as his sister would have been, others as old as his mother was when she passed. All pencil sketches had dates and the same signature: a delicate white campion, the grave flower. Before he could make sense of any of that, Georgia let out a sigh and poured two glasses of a thick green liquor. They pushed one towards Kinglsey: absinth, a spirit he had quit a long time ago. The fox downed theirs, and seeing that the man wouldn't touch his, they downed the unwanted glass too.

"I thought I had it under control."

The words floated like dying leaves, meaningless and yet threatening. Kinglsey looked in the same direction as the kizune: a portrait hung on the wall, in all appearances similar to the countless others. The fox stood up and removed the pins that held the paper in place. They stroked the drawn face, and Kinglsey understood the origin of the blurry pencil lines. The spots and wrinkles too; a tear landed on the visage before Georgia crushed the parchment in their fist. They clutched it so hard that Kingsley heard the knuckles crack. The sound broke the reverie. Georgia wiped their humid eyes and, with extreme care, flattened the portrait back into its original shape.

"She was the last one I helped. Raped by her husband. She came to me to be free of the twisted seed he planted in her. I don't know why she was different, what made her regret her decision last minute, but she did."

They paused, poured two other glasses, and drank both of them straight before continuing.

"Juniper—that's the name she shouted as I was eating the years of her unborn child. She named the fucking child! She named it!"

Madness blurred the amber eyes of the old fox when they hit the table with both fists. Kinglsey remained silent, unsure what to say. Georgia took the liquor bottle and gulped down the rest of the spirit.

"Kinglsey, in your years of 'adventure', have you ever encountered a Nightmare?"

The question was obviously rhetorical. Although he had not, he knew enough to understand the gravity of the situation.

"That bitch—she birthed one that night. Misshapen Ectoplasm of her unborn son. She somehow decided that her husband loved her and that this son would be the solution to all of her misfortune. *Ha. Ha.* What a joke! In the blink of an eye, she forgot the violence, the hits and names, the bruises on her skin and soul, and for what? The hope of a loving household? A fucking lie, I'll tell ya! A fucking lie!"

With nothing to drink, they left Kingsley in the room and returned with another bottle. Floating in the yellow liquid, a hellhornet as big as a finger, which Georgia swallowed in the first sip without hesitation.

"Anyway, she died. Good riddance. I don't think I would have had the heart to help her after her sick husband had knocked her up again. But she left me a gift, right? So I would remember her and fucking Juniper, the unborn bastard! The Nightmare engulfed her straightaway, swallowing whatever was left of her and leaving no bones nor flesh behind. You, blood cultists, you know what it is, aye? You know the price to kill an Ectoplasm of Regrets, right? Well, I didn't. At least not at that time. So, I sealed it."

They sat down heavily in the big chair, swallowed by its cushions.

"I sacrificed my power to anchor the aberration, and I named that forsaken place the Whispering Woods to honour the unborn children whose voices were lost before anyone could ever hear them. Yes, Kinglsey, don't look at me like that; it was aeons ago, when Dewneedin was but a small town called Woodhoff, way before your great, great, great, and great-great grandfathers and mothers even walked this land. Soon, the people I knew died, and unable to perform my craft, my reputation got lost in time. The Whispering Woods became a myth—a haunted place of unspeakable evil wonders that adventurers decided to explore. I sacrificed my powers, but I still maintain the magic around the anchor. And until a couple of weeks ago, I had it under control."

The bottle of hellhornet liquor was empty, and Georgia stood silent for a moment. Kingsley, shocked by the revelations, knew the task given to him would not be easy.

"Kingsley, whatever that kid did cannot be undone. You need to kill it."

## 4. WHERE EVIL LIES…

The first rays of the sun passed through the window, bathing Lilly's face with a golden light that enhanced the honey colour of her skin. She woke up as fresh as a flower. In comparison, the lack of sleep had carved bags under Kingsley's eyes and his worries still inhabited his very soul. His wife embraced him, naked and rotund. He held her close, closer than he could but never close enough for his liking. He felt a kick from Sullivan and burst into tears.

"My love, I know you swore not to wield it again and that you are a man of honour. But whatever Georgia told you last night, it needs to be addressed or it will devour you for the rest of your life. I don't need to know. *Shh.*"

She pressed her fingers on his lips and their calluses reminded him of how wonderful she was, a talented woodcarver that Fate had put on his path. He respected her boundaries and kept the twisted story to himself.

"I will go home as Georgia demanded. They never did such a thing, so I figured the danger is real. I'll trust them and, most importantly, I trust you. Last night, I carved this, for luck."

She handed him an oval item with runes sculpted on its surface. The ebony was heavy in his hand and Kinglsey knew the wood was imbued with magic.

"If you are in great perils, use it. Sullivan is the command word. The runes will teleport you right back to me. To us."

They held each other tighter than before, and their intimacy was interrupted by a knock on the door. Kinglsey took his hammer, kissed his wife and left.

\*\*\*

The gravel road to Albert's cottage was tricky, even for Fern. The steep path led them to the abandoned house. The door was opened but the lock intact, dust covered the furniture and a rotten meal left on the table fostered its own ecosystem. Flies buzzed everywhere, so big Kingsley would not have been surprised to find a corpse in one of the rooms.

"It is as I left it, two weeks ago, when I saw Ivy for the last time."

Georgia's voice was croaky, and they held their skull to massage the hangover away.

Footsteps were visible in the dust, three different sets: paws, Georgia's; small feet, probably the kid's; and adult-sized, surely

Albert's. Some were fresher than others but definitely weeks old. Kinglsey made his way to the back rooms and started searching the father's chambers. After a quick search, he found an old journal. Before he could read it, Georgia laid a paw on his hand.

"Remember, no soul is left untouched by evil. Albert was no exception. Read the diary if you wish but don't let this cloud your judgement. He was grieving his wife, navigating the pain the best he could. Decent man, terrible father."

Kingsley decided to wait before diving into Albert's privacy.

Ivy's room as messy as one can expect. Being the kid of a toy maker, the shelves were filled with dusty puppets, dolls and carved creatures. Metal gears and wires would set in motion incredible pieces of engineering, designed to entertain children or amaze customers. The work was intricate, no magic involved, like nothing he had seen before. The room revealed no clues of interest, until Kinglsey went to the wardrobe. If he hid his most valuable item behind planks, why couldn't a kid do the same? Pushing aside the few coats and robes, he found it, Ivy's most precious possession: a drawing.

Peering from behind, Georgia let out a sob.

Drawn with charcoal, a child holding his father's hand. The man, facing the skies, had tears on his face. But most surprisingly, the boy had another kid drawn on his stomach.

"Judith died in labour. My midwives had told her she awaited twins, but when we opened her up, we rescued only one babe, Ivy. It is rare but not unseen. One of the twins ate the other or fused together in a single being. No one in the village knows, but Albert made sure that Ivy never interacts with people. You'll read it in the journal."

As the fox spoke, they held a pendant: a little white flower, very similar to a white campion.

***

*I should name him Ivy, like the poison he is.*

As a future father, Kingsley couldn't help but despise the man who wrote those words about his only son. Sure, his beloved died but the baby was not responsible for Fate, only the fruit of it. Putting such guilt on a child was inhuman, evil. No wonder the poor boy went into the Whispering Woods without hesitation!

The rest of the journal sickened the old adventurer. Neglect, verbal violence, from all evidence, Ivy did not grow up in a loving household. A dark part of Kinglsey's soul wished Albert had suffered a painful death, but the man recognised the voice and its wicked thoughts. Ever since he had read the diary, his hammer had spoken to him louder than usual, the ruby glowing as bright as the sun. Whatever evil lay in those woods, he would crush it and feed it to the weapon for it to shut up.

"Kingsley, there is something I did not tell you."

His heart stopped. He didn't know if he could handle any more of this. He looked down at the sad fox, expecting them to be smoking or drinking their sorrow away. They weren't.

"Before he disappeared, Albert ate at the inn every night. Never drank, only ate. But one day, he ordered a full bottle of hellhornet and finished it faster than I would have. He stood even after the last call bell, so I sat down with him. 'She's alive,' he said to me, 'Viv, my daughter. Ivy found her in the woods. At first, I did not believe him, but he insisted, so I followed him past the white campion clearing, up to the ruins of an ancient house, and she was there! And Judith too! Oh Georgia, the relief! You can't imagine what it feels like to let go of your anger and grief, put it down at your feet and hold your family in your arms. I felt the love warming my cold carcass and beside me, Ivy smiled. God, I love that child, he is the spitting image of Judith...' He left me with those words and the next day, Ivy took the meal in the forest."

Kinglsey observed the woods, trying to locate evidence of the Nightmare that inhabited them, but he knew the voice would guide him better than his eyes. He left Fern and Georgia, walked down the hill, and penetrated the Whispering Woods.

## 5. AND DARKNESS GROWS...

The canopy hid the sun and stole the warmth of the air in an instant. Kinglsey's skin prickled with goose bumps—from the cold or fear, he was not sure. All he knew was that behind him, Dewneedin could be in danger if he left the Nightmare roaming freely. The wind blowing through the leaves gave a new meaning to the Whispering Woods. It was like thousands of tiny voices murmuring nonsense, ghosts from another time, ancient stories long forgotten.

With each step, his courage grew thinner. The forest felt like a void, sucking the life out of you and replacing it with dread. Shadows from dead trees moved with the wind, like spectres in the night. Why on earth would a child willingly venture into such a terrifying place?

After what felt like hours, Kingsley finally arrived in a clearing, bathed in the light of the zenith sun. The contrast between the darkness behind him and the luminosity in front overwhelmed his eyes, and for a moment he had to squint them so tight that he could barely see any more. When his pupils got accustomed to the light, Kingsley discovered a place of pure delight in the mist of the hellish woods: white flowers like a carpet, grass so green only a painter could do it justice and most important of all, the graves. Headstones, delicately carved with intricate designs, sprouted like saplings among the flowers. Butterflies, hoverflies and bees seemed to be the only visible inhabitants of this place, curiously silent, as if isolated from the rest of the world by a sacred veil or a magical dome.

Kingsley carefully walked through the clearing, avoiding the delicate flowers, and creating a path in the untouched grass. He observed each tomb with curiosity and respect, intrigued by the absence of names and dates. Moss or lichen did not grow on the polished stones, or maybe someone made sure it wouldn't, which made the place even more mystical. How come nobody knew about this cemetery?

Halfway through, Kingsley felt uneasy, as if observed by a hidden predator on the hunt. Only then did he realise that he had not been feeling cold or afraid while wandering in this safe haven. The curse of the woods had somehow lifted; the air was fresh and breathable, but now, the shadows crept once more. A cloud passed through the blue sky and hid the sun, an omen of evil lurking over him. He continued, bracing himself for danger, the handle of his hammer bumping on his shoulder as he walked out of the clearing.

If leaving the darkness of the woods overwhelmed his eyes, it was at least reassuring to see light again. Diving into the darkness was like suffering the weight of Time itself, crushing each of Kinglsey's bones and hopes. A glance back, and fear iced his veins: the cemetery had gone, vanished, swallowed by creaking trees covered in vines. Along with the fears, the goosebumps were back, and Kingsley rapidly forgot the warmth of the sun he felt not so long ago.

The rest of the journey dragged, with time and space as

flexible as bread dough, stretched by an evil baker. Kingsley pulled out a scone that Georgia had left him, but the snack tasted like ashes in his mouth. He bit into the juicy apple, hoping the refreshing fruit would wake his drowsy mind, but the flesh was powdery and bland. He sat down on a boulder and put his face in his trembling hands. Sorrow and grief from unknowable losses possessed his heart, mistreating it relentlessly and lashing it with whips as sharp as a million knives. Then the voice spoke.

*Kinglsey, o my Kinglsey. Listen to those crying babies, whose lungs never functioned, whose voice never filled the air. Sullivan could have been one of them. Maybe Lilly came here to get rid of him, like all those ungrateful mothers. Mothers? No, murderers! Life is a gift! Blood is a gift! Why would you kill something so beautiful and sacred? At least, wait for them to be born so I could feast on their souls, crush their skulls and drink the life out of them... What a waste.*

*Kinglsey, trust me. I only care about you, giving you the life you deserve. Follow my directions, and you shall find what you call a Nightmare. Trust me, and you shall see the beauty where no one else can: a collection of lost souls swirling together in a powerful entity. Regrets, pain and despair, all dancing together within the Nightmare. You will see, my friend, and you will feed them to me.*

## 6. IF INNOCENCE IS AT RISK...

Kingsley walked straight, in a trance, paying no attention to any of his surroundings. He tumbled on rocks, rolled his ankle twice and even swallowed a fly, but he did not care; the path was laid before him, and he only had to walk. The voice kept him company. Walking, he forgot why he was there in the first place. He had forgotten about Ivy, the village and the danger. What mattered was feeding the hammer, and pleasing the voice, like he used to ages ago.

Memories of a former life floated in his mind, merged with the present like a caricature of his reality. The human-shaped tree became a devoted zealot, ready to give up his life for the Cult; the bush on his right, a chest full of the donations from Cultists; the red flowers on the grass looked like all the blood he had spilled.

Suddenly, gravel replaced the forest humus. Somehow, this change took him back to the now. It could have been the sound of his boots crunching on the sand and tiny rocks or the smell of the roses that grew on the house before him like dark veins on ageing, pale skin, but it was the voice of a kid that anchored him back in reality.

"Dad? Is that you?"

The child was thin—sickly thin. Dark circles underneath his young eyes, blueish lips like two slugs on a pale face. The blond or white hair gathered in a high ponytail, flew with the breeze, and Kingsley wondered how the wind did not blow the whole kid away, like a kite on Junimo's day. All wrapped up in rags, the child walked towards him, barefoot, arms wide open.

"Wait... You're not Dad! Who are you?"

The feeble shoulders sagged as the kid backed.

"You are here to kill, aren't you? You're here to kill my sister! You murderer!"

Kingsley had to quickly duck to avoid the rock, but a second one hit him in the chest. The child ran to the half-crumbled door and slid inside the ruin, out of sight.

Still in shock, Kingsley took a few steps backward to

observe the building: two-storey, collapsed on one side, the house was from a time when walls were made of dry stones stacked on top of each other. The roof, made of black slate tiles, still covered most of the ruin, thanks to the quality of the wood framework. The windows had no glass, but raised panels were used to prevent any trespasser. Now, the shutters hung miserably on creaky hinges.

Kingsley noticed a shadow passing while looking at the rose vines growing inside the house through one of the upstairs windows. With the warhammer in his hands, he pushed the door open with the head of the weapon. With a wet sound, the weapon pierced a hole in the wood, freeing xylophages. He looked at the bugs crawling in the wood mush before carefully sliding through the hole like the kid did, trying not to step on any of the peaceful beetles.

Inside, the smell of rot and decay kept him vigilant. Although one wall had collapsed, it felt like he was trapped in a shrinking room. In front of him were a flight of stairs, overgrown by moss and probably as stable as his mental strength. He explored the rest of the ground floor, but no trace of the kid. No trace of the Nightmare either. Back to the mouldy staircase, Kinglsey saw darker stains amongst the green moss. With caution, he climbed up, only putting his feet in the footsteps left by a much lighter and agile child.

Two times he thought everything would collapse under him; two times the wood held his weight with a squeaking noise. On the last steps, he let down his guard, too eager to reach the second floor, and his leg passed through the wood. Losing his balance, he grabbed the handrail, which crumbled into his fist. Gravity grasped him, trying to tie him back to the ground. With his left hand still holding the hammer, Kingsley managed to hook the weapon to the floor. He was now hanging from the handle, miraculously anchored in the hard floor. He heard the rest of the staircase collapse, and a heavy cloud of dust and mould rose from the ground.

"Here, let me help you, sir."

A tiny hand appeared, and without thinking twice, Kingsley swung to reach it. Both grunting, the kid finally managed to pull him up, and they both stayed speechless for their lungs cried for air. When they had caught their breath, the child stood up and gave him another helping hand. Back on his feet, Kingsley realised how lanky the kid was, like a twig. He thanked him and pulled out the hammer from the floor.

"What an impressive weapon! Are you an adventurer? I'm sorry about earlier; I shouldn't have called you names... Maybe you are here to help!"

Like his son will do in the future, the kid took Kingsley by the wrist and showed him the way.

## 7. ONE CAN LOSE CONTROL...

It was but a small room with sunrays filtering through the old shutters and dust suspended in the air like fairy lights. Some straw was piled up in a corner, next to a bucket and an empty plate. By the smell of the room, Kinglsey knew that the kid remained mostly inside. Sweat, human waste and rotten food, odours of a prison cell that brought back unpleasant memories. The hammer fed on Kingsley's discomfort, and the ruby glowed a little stronger.

"That is a very impressive weapon, sir! Can I see?"

Before he could say anything, the kid grabbed the handle and lifted the heavy hammer like it was made of wood. He swung it effortlessly, wielding it like an experienced warrior. Kingsley knew the curse and hoped the voice did not talk to the child, whispering its sweet promises of incredible adventures. He grabbed the weapon and put a hand on the kid's shoulder.

"You are too young to wield a weapon like this, boy. Trust me, enjoy your innocence while you can. Fate is a twisted thing, and one never knows when it will turn. Are you Ivy?"

A frown wrinkled the child's forehead, and he stomped off to his straw bed.

"Grown-ups are all the same, always spoiling the fun. You're like Dad."

Those words hit Kingsley right in the heart as he remembered the diary. He looked at the child brooding in his corner with extreme empathy. Suddenly, the air became heavy, and the sun disappeared. The old adventurer noticed something moving on the wall opposite the door, like shadows. Before his eyes, black spots started moving on the stones, fusing together into a large circle. Then, the whole darkness trickled off the wall and oozed its way to the centre of the room.

The Ectoplasm was smaller than Kinglsey had expected. He let out a sigh of relief and took his hammer, ready to destroy the abomination. The black blob turned its... head? towards him, and pseudopods sprouted from its side like ink tentacles. Kinglsey braced himself for impact, but the creature did not attack. The oozy arms, dripping with shadowy matter, splashed on the floor and disconnected themselves from the main entity into puddles of black slime. In a disgusting slushing sound, Lilly and teenage Sullivan stood in front of Kinglsey, goo-clones of his most beloved people.

"My love, I am glad you are here! We've been waiting for you!"

"Dad, why did you leave for so long? I missed you…"

His wife's voice was the same, except for a slight wetness in the consonants. His boy looked so much like him at his age, Kinglsey felt his eyes watering. This couldn't be… Sullivan was still a babe in the womb; how could he be old enough to drink ale, and yet Lilly looked younger than she does now and pregnant?

*O Kinglsey, my poor soul, don't you understand? This is what you could have had if you had never joined the Cult. Your son would be fifteen, and your wife awaiting the birth of another child. Your choices led you to this, and the Ectoplasm is showing you what to regret.*

Lilly split in two, and the goo shaped another kid next to her: a toddler with long curls, holding its no-longer-pregnant mother's hand. Queasiness squeezed his guts, and Kingsley felt the hammer pumping his life-essence.

In the background, shadows kept crawling and fusing into the Nightmare, until it became too large for the height of the ceiling. Kingsley, hypnotised by his gooey fake-family, only noticed the threat when the Ectoplasm engulfed his creations in a wet noise. For a split second, Lilly smiled at her husband before being swallowed back to where she came from.

Seeing his wife disappear, Kingsley's heart stopped, and a terrible ache compressed his chest. He had only one wish: follow her, follow them, even if it meant the death of him. Before he could step forward into the black hole, the hammer spoke with haste.

*Where do you think you're going, Kingsley? You must feed me first! Kill the child.*

Eyes glowing red like rubies, the adventurer turned around

and looked at the kid on his straw bed, seemingly unaware of the gigantic Nightmare next to them.

One step, the hammer tightly secured in his grasp. Two steps, arms up in the air. Three steps, ruby glowing like blood. Four steps, the weapon dropping on the vulnerable skull of an innocent child... But, to the cursed hammer's surprise, the Ectoplasm formed a protective shield around the boy just before impact. The weapon landed on the shadow goo and lost its control over Kingsley's mind.

Back to his senses, the adventurer took no time to dwell on his mistake and swung the hammer with all his strength. The metal head hit the Ectoplasm behind him, and black ink splashed everywhere.

In a cry of despair, the kid stood up and launched himself onto Kinglsey, trying to prevent the next attack.

"No! Don't hurt them! Please! Stop!"

The child didn't weigh much, and Kinglsey swung a second time, as threatening pseudopods had already sprouted from the Nightmare, ready to strike. His sudden movement made the kid lose his grip on his arm, and the child landed harshly on the floor. Another drop of black ooze splashed on Kinglsey's shoulder. From the various puddles splattered around, more pseudopods grew until the whole room looked like a demonic octopus. With his bare hand, Kingsley squeezed the one growing on his shoulder, and the tiny tentacle vanished in a cry that sounded like Lilly's. A wave of utter regret filled Kinglsey's soul.

*Kill the kid, Kingsley! Then I will be able to feed on the Nightmare!*

Resisting the urge to obey, the adventurer swung the weapon recklessly until he was surrounded by puddles too numerous to count. Then, the Ectoplasm changed shape: it retracted onto the walls, as thin as it could be to avoid the attacks. It was like being surrounded by darkness, almost impossible to see your surroundings, for the only dim light came from the cursed ruby.

"Boy? Where are you?"

No response.

"Ivy? Please, I'm here to take you home."

The Nightmare shapeshifted into his massive round form again, and the sudden light blinded Kinglsey, who dropped the weapon to cover his eyes. When the man could finally see the kid, eyes glowing red, was ready to crush his skull with the hammer.

Kingsley dropped and rolled on his side, barely avoiding the deathly hit. On the ground, he managed to grapple the legs of the kid and pull them towards him. Loosing balance, the child toggled and fell. Three pseudopods wrapped around the unconscious boy before Kinglsey could do anything to prevent it.

Groggy, the adventurer watched the black goo shapeshift into three humans, cuddling the kid in a loving embrace, and he understood. In his loneliness, Ivy had found a family, and there was no way convincing him otherwise. As much as he wanted to rescue the child, he knew he had to use the hammer's power. Hitting the Nightmare only delayed the inevitable: all the goo was already fused back into the main entity. Kinglsey had to kill Ivy.

## 8. AND WIELD GUILT AND REGRETS...

Unaware of Kinglsey's intentions, Ivy still enjoyed his family's embrace. The adventurer, fire in his eyes, approached stealthily, somehow surprised that the Ectoplasm wouldn't attack him to protect its anchor. From what he knew, Nightmares needed a willing creature as a plane-anchor, and Ivy must have sacrificed some of his soul to be bound to the entity. Georgia had said it was a Nightmare of Regrets, so whatever Ivy did, it must have been done with genuine and hurtful regrets.

Shifting anchors wasn't something Kinglsey had done before, but the theory was simple enough: destroy the previous anchor in an act of similar power. In this case, killing Ivy with regrets as strong as the sacrifice he had done. On top of that, Kinglsey had to kill the boy to trigger the hammer's curse. The weapon, infused with blood and death, would swallow the Nightmare, and trap it inside. There was no other way.

He lifted the weapon. He could already feel tears rolling from his eyes. It was like killing his own son. Unable to cope with the guilt, he turned his face before bringing down the deadly hammer.

A burst of light shone, and someone cried. Kinglsey could feel warm blood on his skin, smell of iron in the air. Slowly, he turned his head to witness, in utter shock, the slaughter he had caused. He braced himself for the anchor shift, whatever that might feel like. But before he could comprehend, Lilly lay in front of him, the hammer empaling her broken skull. In her hand, she was holding a familiar wooden sculpture with luminous runes.

In a wail that could have opened a gate to the Seven Hells, Kingsley became the new anchor. In fury, he let the cursed weapon take control and swung like a madman. Instead of splashing goo everywhere, the Ectoplasm was sucked inside the hammer, until there was nothing left of it. Kinglsey continued to hit the walls and floor, uncapable of coping with the suffering that consumed his very core. When he had nothing left to destroy, he dropped to his knees close to his dead wife.

The red in his eyes was no longer the curse but the result of his tears. He replaced a curl of hair behind Lilly's ear and removed the crimson smear on her cheek. Sobbing, he held her corpse in his arms and let his sorrow echo in the silence.

After what seemed like an eternity, Kinglsey realised that Lilly's body felt and smelled different. He looked at her face. No, it was her, and he put his palm on her belly, hoping to feel Sullivan's kicks. He didn't feel anything—not because the babe was dead, but because his wife wasn't pregnant! He put his second hand and touched what used to be a nine-month-pregnant belly, only to feel the flatness of it. And, as if his realisation triggered something, the glamour surrounding his wife faded. In his arms, Georgia's corpse laid peacefully.

### 9. Until Hope Is Born

Kingsley walked into the corridor, impatient and worried. Lilly's cries resonated in the whole building and nothing could ease his concerns. Lost in his dark thoughts, he paced like a caged lion until Ivy grabbed his hand.

"She will be all right, and soon you will be the dad of a beautiful son!"

Kinglsey dropped to his knees and held the child tightly. Ivy had gained weight in the past three weeks and looked healthier than the twiggy kid he had rescued. The old adventurer let his emotions out, and his adoptive son smiled while patting Kinglsey's back.

After a couple of minutes, the wailing stopped. Immediately, Kinglsey stood on his feet, burst into the room and froze in place. The midwife was holding a crying new-born; his son, Sullivan.

He approached his wife, but Lilly let out another wail. The midwife gave the baby to Kinglsey and tended to her patient.

"Twins! Congratulations! This one is a girl!"

Ivy let out a cry of joy and ran to the bed to see the midwife cutting the umbilical cord. Kinglsey, still in shock, looked deeply into Sullivan's half-closed eyes as the baby grabbed one of his dad's fingers in his small hand.

Ivy, smiling at the little girl, said to his parents, "I know how we could name her! She could be Hope, a living proof that the future is always brighter than we think, that Fate always rewards the people in need. What do you say?"

Kinglsey looked up at his wife, smiling, and he nodded.

"I think it is a wonderful name, Ivy! And I believe that you will be the greatest brother to them."

Lilly's voice was still tainted with fatigue. Sweat glistening on her temples, and her cheeks were red as ripe apples. The midwife carefully placed both babies on Lilly's bare breast, and the mother stroked their wrinkled faces with tenderness. She then gestured Kinglsey to come closer. Holding Ivy's hand in hers, she closed her eyes and sighed.

"We will carry Georgia's sacrifice for the rest of our lives, but she did not die in vain. She chose her destiny and redemption by giving her life to rescue ours and countless others."

They all looked at each other, grateful to be here together, alive and well. They gathered on the bed with the twins in the middle, all amazed by the two little creatures. Kinglsey cried silently and kissed Lilly's forehead. For some reason, his neck felt warm, and he held the white campion pendant in a silent thank you.